THE GIVING TREE

The Giving Tree

by

Shel Silverstein

HarperCollinsPublishers

THE GIVING TREE

For information address HarperCollins Children's Books, a division of HarperCollins Publishers, 1350 Avenue of the Americas, New York, NY 10019.
www.harperchildrens.com

Library of Congress catalog card number: 64-11840
ISBN-10: 0-06-025665-6 (trade bdg.) — ISBN-13: 978-0-06-025665-4 (trade bdg.)
ISBN-10: 0-06-025666-4 (lib. bdg.) — ISBN-13: 978-0-06-025666-1 (lib. bdg.)
Special Holiday Edition:
ISBN-10: 0-06-084098-6 (trade bdg.) — ISBN-13: 978-0-06-084098-3 (trade bdg.)

37 38 39 40 ❖ First Edition

For
Nicky

Once there was a tree…

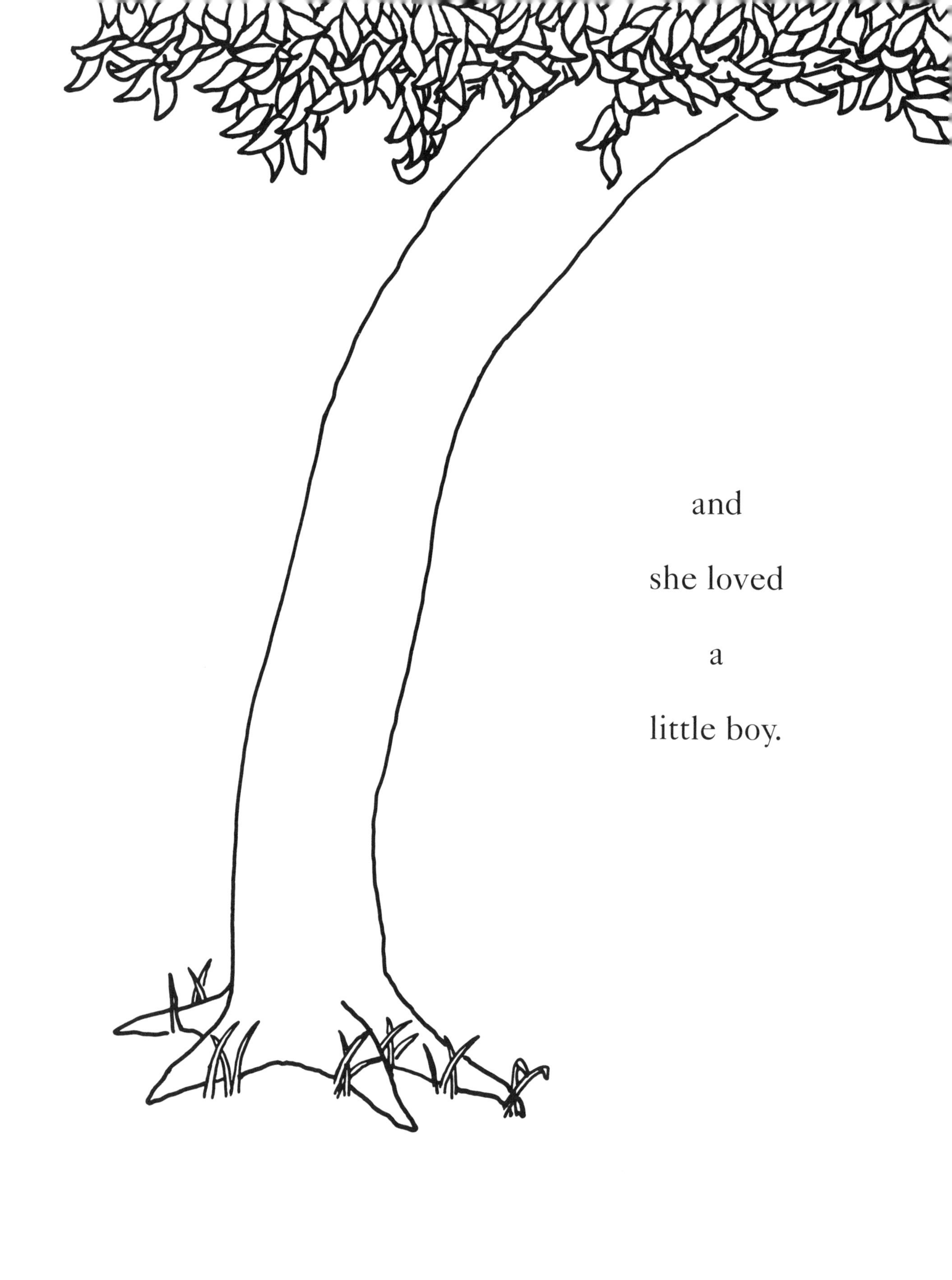

and

she loved

a

little boy.

And every day
the boy
would come

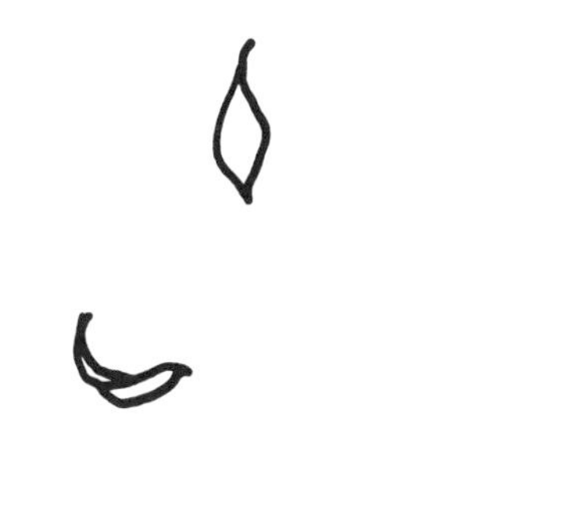

and

he

would

gather

her

leaves

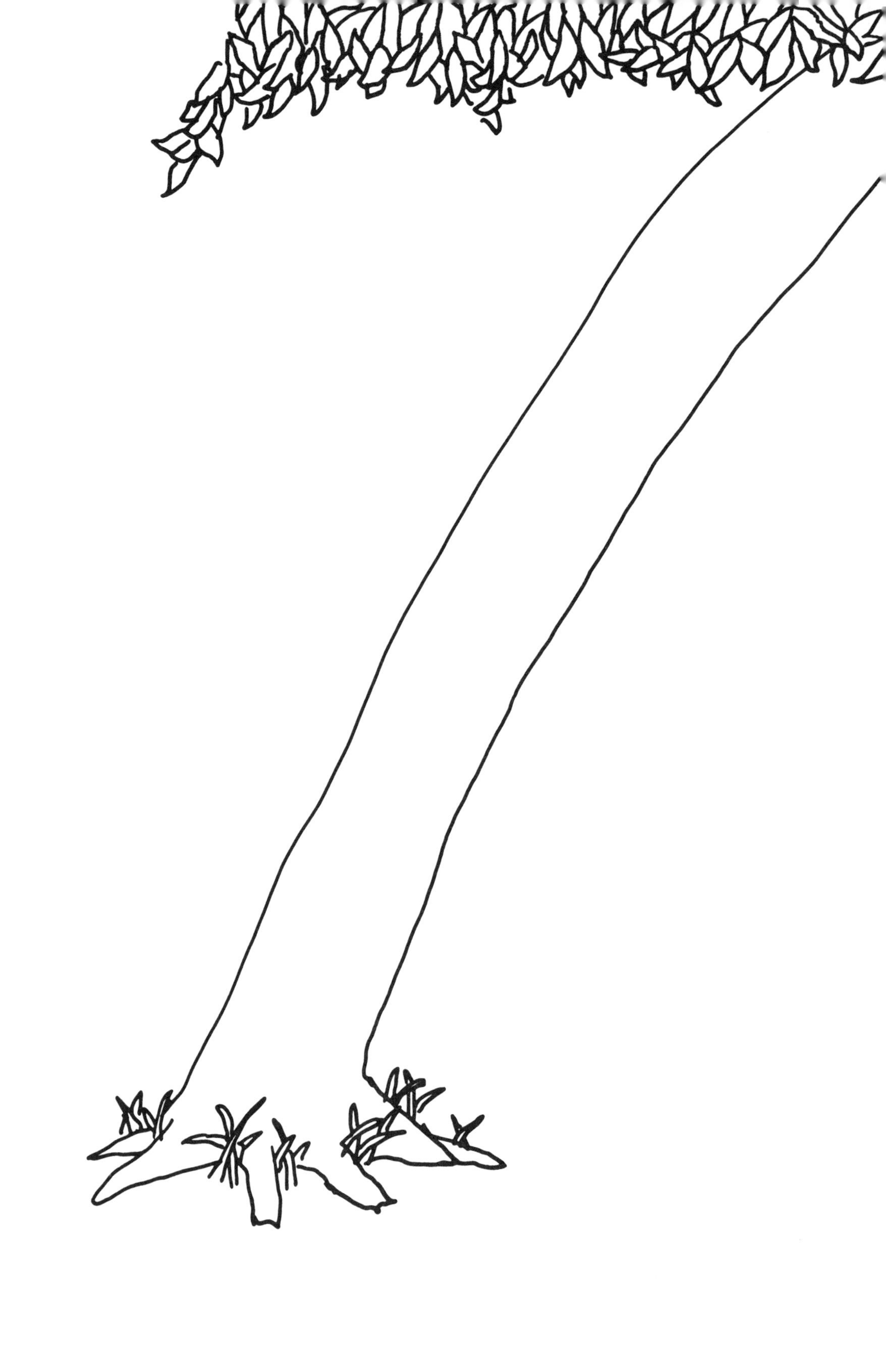

and make them
into crowns
and play king of the forest.

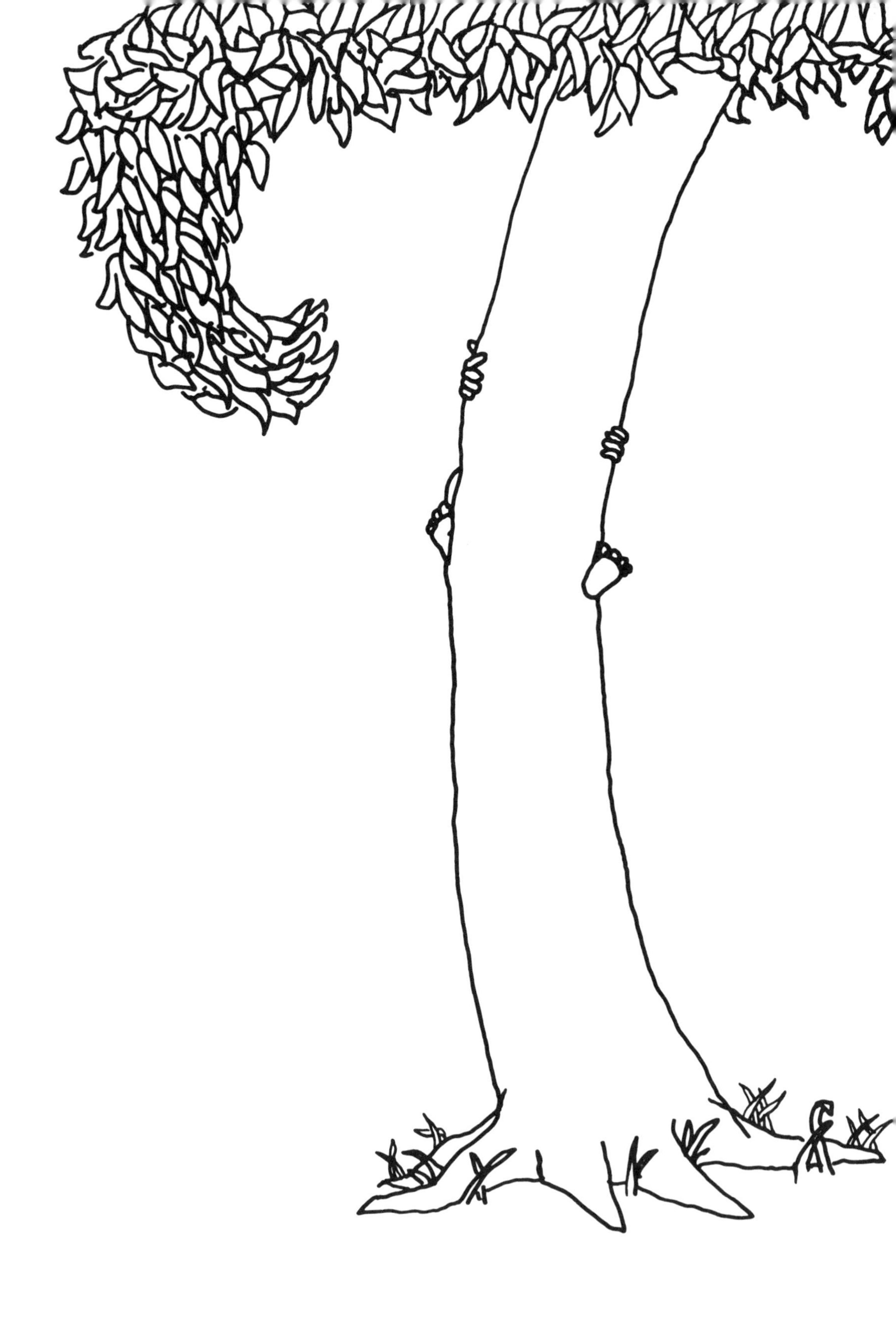

He would climb up her trunk

and swing from her branches

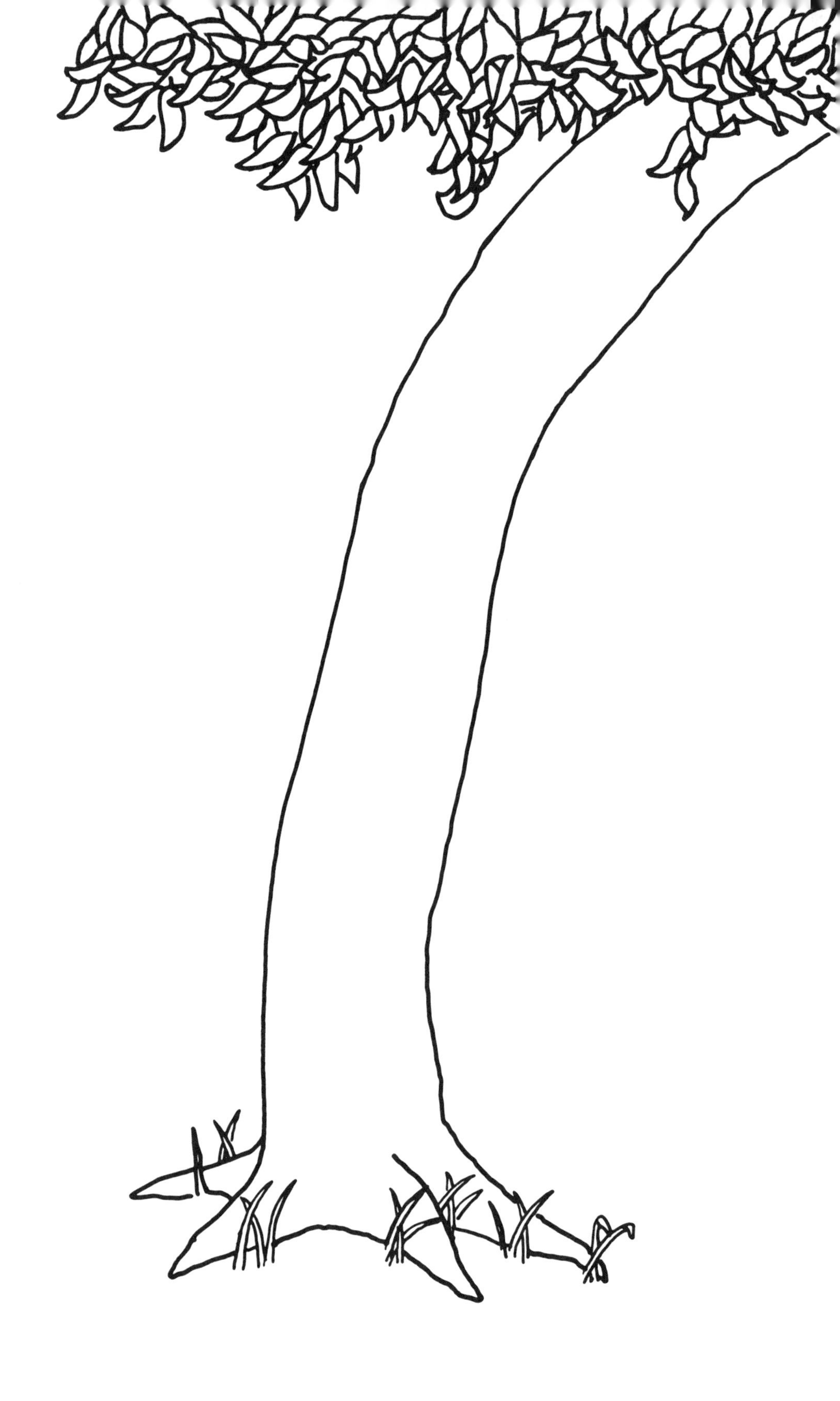

and eat apples.

And they
would play
hide-and-go-seek.

And when
he was tired,
he would sleep
in her shade.

And the boy loved the tree . . .

very much.

And the tree was happy.

M.E.
+
T.

But time went by.

M.E. & Y.L.
M.E. & T.

And the boy grew older.

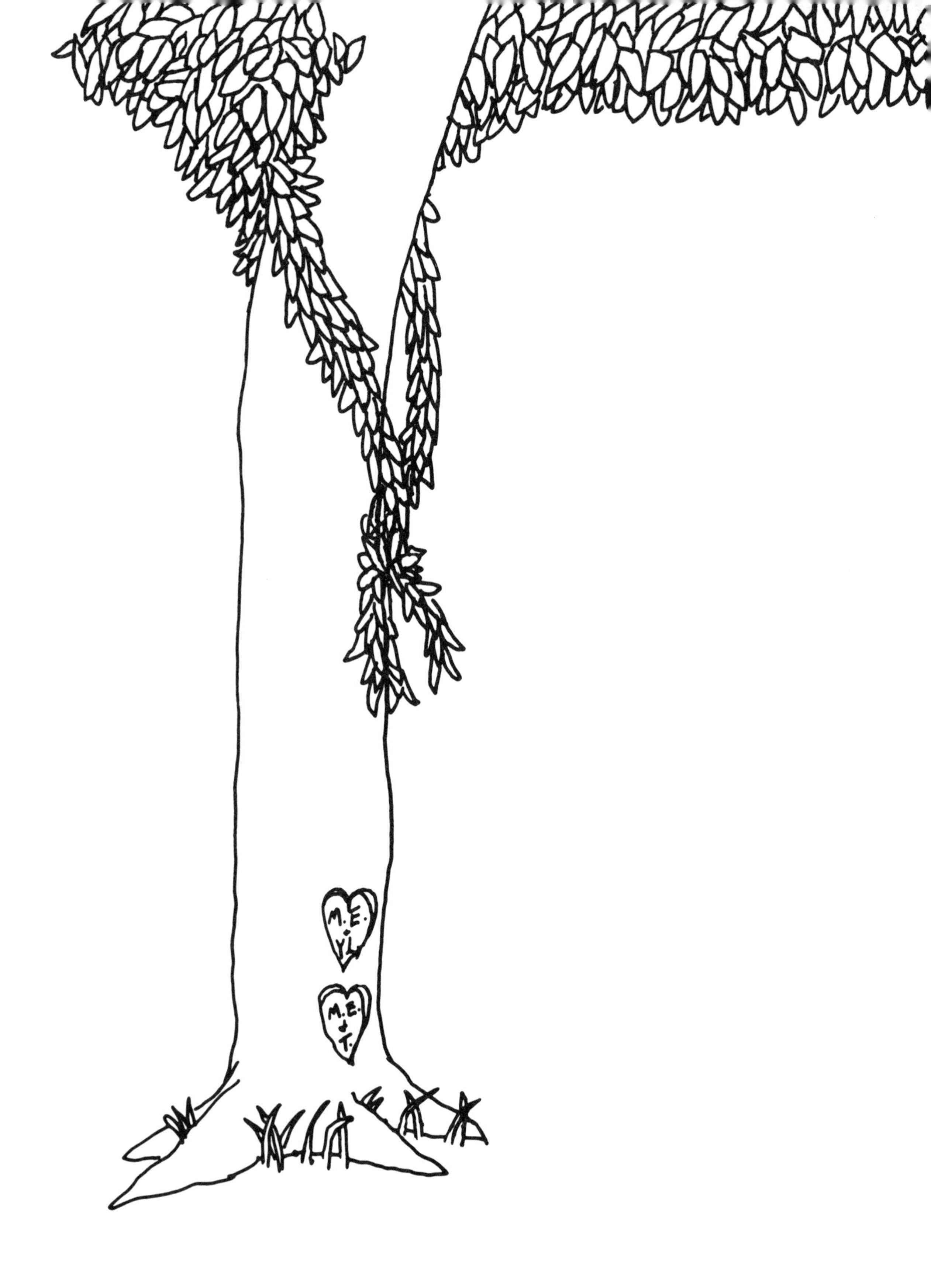
M.E.
Y.L.
M.E.
&
T.

And the tree was often alone.

Then one day the boy came to the tree
and the tree said, "Come, Boy, come and climb
up my trunk and swing from my branches
and eat apples and play in my shade
and be happy."
"I am too big to climb and play," said the boy.
"I want to buy things and have fun.
I want some money.
Can you give me some money?"
"I'm sorry," said the tree, "but I have no money.
I have only leaves and apples.
Take my apples, Boy, and sell them
in the city. Then you will have money
and you will be happy."

M.E. + Y.L.
M.E. + T.

M.E. + Y.L.
M.E. + T.

And so the boy climbed up the
tree and gathered
her apples
and carried them away.

And the tree was happy.

But the boy stayed away
for a long time . . .
and the tree was sad.
And then one day
the boy came back
and the tree shook with joy
and she said, "Come, Boy,
climb up my trunk
and swing from my branches
and be happy."

"I am too busy to climb trees,"
said the boy.
"I want a house to keep me warm,"
he said.
"I want a wife and I want children,
and so I need a house.
Can you give me a house?"
"I have no house," said the tree.
"The forest is my house,
but you may cut off my branches
and build a house.
Then you will be happy."

And so the boy cut off
her branches
and carried them away
to build his house.

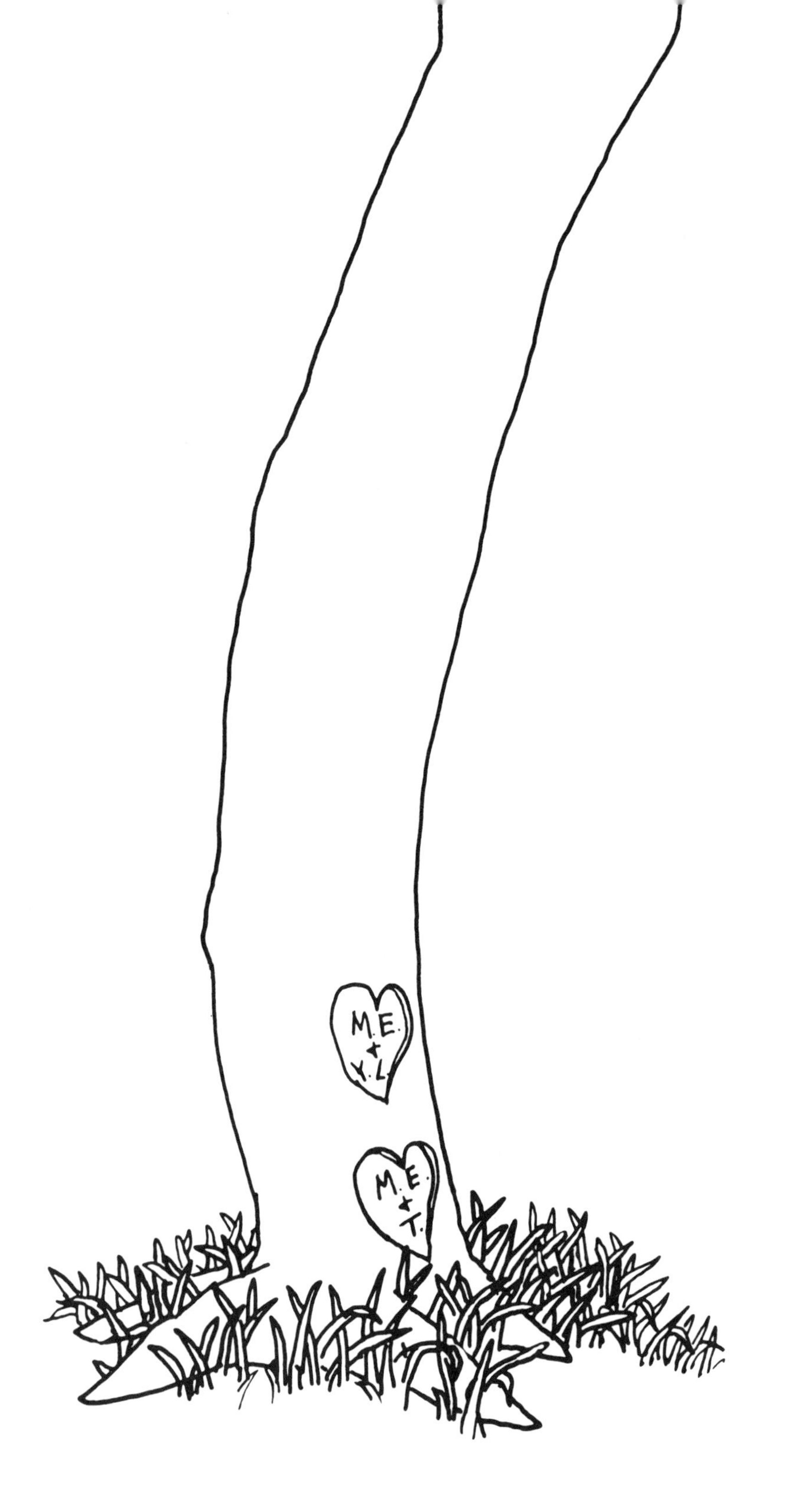
M.E. + Y.L.
M.E. + T.

And the tree was happy.

But the boy stayed away
for a long time.
And when he came back,
the tree was so happy
she could hardly speak.
“Come, Boy,” she whispered,
“come and play.”
“I am too old and sad to play,”
said the boy.
“I want a boat that will
take me far away
from here.
Can you give me a boat?”

"Cut down my trunk
and make a boat,"
said the tree.
"Then you can sail away...
and be happy."

And so the boy cut down her trunk

and made a boat and sailed away.

And the tree was happy . . .

but not really.

And after a long time
the boy came back again.
"I am sorry, Boy,"
said the tree, "but I have nothing
left to give you—

My apples are gone."
"My teeth are too weak
for apples," said the boy.
"My branches are gone,"
said the tree. "You
cannot swing on them—"
"I am too old to swing
on branches," said the boy.
"My trunk is gone," said the tree.
"You cannot climb—"
"I am too tired to climb," said the boy.
"I am sorry," sighed the tree.
"I wish that I could
give you something...
but I have nothing left. I am just
an old stump. I am sorry...."

"I don't need very much now,"
said the boy,
"just a quiet place to sit and rest.
I am very tired."
"Well," said the tree,
straightening herself up
as much as she could,
"well, an old stump *is* good
for sitting and resting.
Come, Boy, sit down.
Sit down and rest."

And the boy did.

And the tree was happy.